secrets of the wild

dustin m. hoffman

word west press | missoula, mt

copyright © 2019 dustin m. hoffman

all rights reserved. no part of this book may be used or reproduced in any manner whatsoever without written permission from the publisher except in the case of brief quotations embodied in critical articles or reviews. for more information, contact word west press.

isbn: 978-1-7334663-2-5

published by word west in missoula, mt.

first us edition 2019.
printed in the usa.

www.wordwest.co

cover image: magda ehlers.
cover & interior design: word west.

For Mom

still life

The kids spotted a giant statue of a buck from the overpass as we trekked upstate on our first family camping trip. The kids demanded we stop. The buck's antlers stretched longer than our sedan, and it could have easily gobbled the engine block and the front seats with its massive muzzle. But deer are vegetarians. This I knew for sure. I figured it couldn't hurt to take the exit and explore this massive gentle beast.

My son, Trent, said the buck must be worth a hundred points. Kay, my wife, laughed. I wanted to correct him, explain that the points had to do with the antlers, not like points in video games. But he'd learn soon enough, once we got up north, where I'd show Trent how to shoot the rifle. There would be a lot of wilderness education on this trip. I had grown up camping, but this was all new to the kids who spent their days cooped inside hovering over glowing screens.

Both of them were possibly geniuses, scoffing at math homework that scared the hair on my back straight. They'd grow up smarter and better than me, with my failing alternator repair shop. And that was great. Really, I was fine with it. But this weekend, I'd be the one to teach them something. Even though money was tight, the trip was worth it. It was my last chance to show my expertise to the kids before I closed up the alternator shop for good and became Father Failure.

Off the exit, we could see the round building under the buck statue's hooves. It was painted an orange as bright as a hunter's safety vest. I was intrigued, and the kids were mesmerized. The statue loomed larger as we approached from behind, its stubby white tail and anus beckoning our adventure off the beaten path of RVs and trailers flashing expensive red motorboats. The kids said, "Can we?" And I said, "Why the hell not?" My wife nuzzled her head against my shoulder, her lips smelling of Dr. Pepper lip balm. We reveled in this precious family-bonding moment of discovering our state's great plaster monuments of tourism. What a state we lived in! Only in Michigan were bucks constructed to match the size of men's full hearts.

Flyers packed the windshield of the only car in the lot. We parked. The kids jumped out and ran around in busy circles, stopping every now and then to hug each other and point at the giant buck on the roof. My wife lifted a flyer from the rusted wiper blade and read it to us: "Whispers of Wilderness. Enter to learn the secret language of the Michigan forest." I pulled another flyer and it was the same. They were all the same.

"Wow," my wife said. "They really sank their advertising budget into the flyers." She taught high school economics.

"Kind of overkill, don't you think," I said, wanting to agree. I thought of my rows of greasy alternators back home. They looked like gorilla fists crowding the shelves. How could I advertise that? I should've listened to her suggestions to diversify with some starters or transmissions. I tried to keep my marketing worries to myself as Judy and Trent sprinted toward the front entrance. A father has a duty to swallow worry.

A taxidermy bear barricaded the front doors. It loomed on its hind legs, teeth exposed and frothy. A slot for money sliced through his paw. Printed on its chest were the words Five-Dollar Admittance. I jammed a twenty into the slot, and there went the s'mores fund. But this was an investment for my kids' education, worth far more than stale marshmallows. After the twenty sucked in, the bear rumbled, "Grrrrrr-ra-rumba-rop, don't forget to visit the gift shop," and slid to the side on a track, his eyes blinking with red lights. We entered.

The lobby was, of course, the gift shop, brightly lit and full of bins spilling plastic deer and bears and loons and wolves and other Michigan wildlife. I didn't see a single person working the counter, which must have kept overhead low but thefts high. Every business choice led to sacrifice. Trent wanted a fox and Judy gripped a doe so tight I thought its head would pop off. I told them that if they were good little fawns they could pick out something later. Kids need to learn to work for rewards.

On the way to the exhibits, we passed a cave trimmed in Styrofoam painted to look like stone. A sign above it warned: Employees Only. A faint red light pulsed from the shadowy entrance. Trent asked what the cave was. I told him, "That's where the animals go for breaks, have some lunch, use the restroom."

"Why don't they just pee outside?" he said.

"Because they have the cave," I said.

That was probably where all the workers were hiding, slacking off, when they could have been selling my kids plastic deer. I pitied the owner, imagined him hunched over a calculator, sweating over the flyer budget, while his workers smoked cigarettes and laughed about his ridiculous ponytail.

Glass cases staggered the dark hallway, displaying still-life tableaus of taxidermy animals. Each case offered hollowed-out bull horns set with speakers that whispered the wild. You could press a button and hold them to your ear to hear the squawks and roars of Michigan's teeming life.

The first diorama featured a bobcat leaping over a felled pine. The kids tucked the bull-horn speakers to their ears, pressed the button, and I heard the muffled whine and hiss of the bobcat, followed by a low, masculine voice, probably explaining a little gem of wisdom or two about the bobcat's behavior or eating habits. Ah, education! I couldn't be happier than for my kids to be learning about their state, knowledge that would give our camping trip more meaning. My wife and I stood behind the kids with our arms wrapped around each other, watching as the bobcat pounced forward on a track. They jumped back. My wife squeezed my butt. We all laughed. I told them that if they ever ran into a real bobcat they should make themselves as big as possible, stretch their arms high over their heads, remind that cat who towered at the top of the food chain. Judy said she would pet the heck out of that cat if she saw it. But then Trent said, "Don't worry, Dad. I'd shoot it right in the tail."

The next cases were smaller: robins perched over their blue-egged nests, hawks swooping on fishing line, two herons rubbing necks. The kids listened to each one carefully, taking turns pressing the buttons. Then there was the snow owl, white and majestic and wise, and when you pressed his button his head spun in a full circle. The kids pushed a bull-horn speaker to my ear, urging me to hear the owl hoot. I broke from my wife and listened, anxious to hear that familiar hooting song from the farm where I'd grown up.

The recording was crackly, distant. I floated with it back to my childhood, could smell the tractor rust, see the pale winter sun cutting through the grayed slats of pine. My parents owned that farm until I was ten, when we moved into the suburbs. My father failed at farming, and then failed at a string of small businesses: a coatrack store, a pillowcase outlet, a ham-only deli. He never figured commerce out, obsessed as he was with fulfilling singular needs. Even with Mom, he'd treated her to the same date of fried perch for two at Famous Ziggy's Tavern every Friday for thirty years.

The owl said, "Whooot-whooo-whooot-Whoo," and then, "Who is that sexy lady with that wild pair of gozangas, and why is she wasting her time with the tubby oaf?"

I pushed the button again. "Whooot-who do you think you are, buddy? Your wife is bored, so why don't you send her in here for a good time."

Who did I think I was? Who the hell was this owl? I could have punched the glass and spun the snow owl's head until it popped right off. No one talked about Kay that way, my best friend, the woman who could melt away the pain of days without a single customer by simply touching my face. But the kids were already running and laughing to the next case. I dropped the bull-horn speaker and stomped after them.

The dark hallways opened up to a scene of huge moose butting heads, their fuzzy antlers interlocked, a cow moose off to the side licking plastic birch trees. I decided to listen with the kids this time, and my wife picked up a speaker too. Trent hit the button. The moose wailed in between simulated antler clunks. And then the masculine voice came through, saying, "Male moose often fight to impress potential mates. But after their mates are secured, ramming passion is replaced by lackluster complacency. It becomes all TV dinners, and the female will be lucky if her cheap mate takes her to a movie twice a year. Sex becomes as banal as hiccups."

The kids sprinted off to the next case. "Can you believe this?" I said to my wife. "What kind of whispers of the wild are these? They're feeding the kids crap sandwiches."

"Honey, not everyone is a wilderness expert like you," she said. "Besides, there's a little bit of truth to it." But I didn't want bits of truth—alternator brushes, diodes, frayed copper wires—I wanted full-on wilderness. She eased a hand around my waist and brought me back. All I needed was for her and the kids to be smiling.

Then came the deer window. The glass was clear as nothing. The kids straightened their backs and prepared to listen again. I went to grab myself a bull-horn speaker, but my wife snagged a belt loop and urged me to just ignore this one. I couldn't resist, though. We had a stake in our kids' futures. We needed to know what they were learning. I needed to know.

A pack of does were frozen in mid bound, a few bucks chasing after. I pushed the button and a fawn slid forward on a track toward the window and then through it, at which point I realized there was no glass on this case. Judy and Trent crowded the doe, stroking its ears, crying about how cute it was. The masculine voice came on: "These days, most deer are hunted by motorists, as they've become impervious to bullets, so there's no use in trying to shoot us, tubb-o. Also, they're the smartest of the mammals, surpassing the far stupider ape family. A little-known fact is that fawns love to eat quarters. Feel free to feed the fawn."

I couldn't wait to show Trent how untrue the bulletproof lie was as soon as we got out of here. The kids tugged on my pant legs, jangling my change, screaming for fawn feed. I wouldn't give in. Even when the jaw dropped to reveal a coin slot, even when my wife tried to keep peace and pass out quarters, I wouldn't submit. I blocked the fawn's hungry slot with my chest, crossed my arms, made myself immovable. I did it for the truth of the wild. Judy started crying. Trent punched my thighs. I told them: no souvenirs then. I pointed toward the exit. And that's where we went, my wife now carrying Judy and Trent stomping out.

We passed the snow hares, the wolves, the bears, the geese. At one point we passed by a small case of penguins, and I tried not to even look at the buffoonery. And then right through the souvenir shop where we'd entered. Judy stopped crying once she saw the plastic does again. How could I deny her? She was my only girl, and it hadn't been her fault. Management was to blame for the lies. Trent got his fox, too. Still there was no one around working the register. I'm no thief, so I left a ten on the counter, which would have been a six-pack to share with my wife, and we headed for the exit.

Instead of the sensor opening the automatic door, a fox dropped from the ceiling. My wife jumped, nearly smacked in the head. Judy whimpered.

"We hope you've enjoyed your visit," the fox said. "Please consider all the lives that ended for you sickos' enjoyment. Maybe you'll consider dying yourself and being stuffed, so we can make a very educational human display. If that doesn't sound so hot, then just consider the choice we had in the matter."

Then the fox's jaw fell open just like the fawn's, revealing another hungry coin slot. Rumbling footsteps echoed from the hallway where the still lifes held their lies. I worried about the deer case without any glass.

My palms sweated around the change in my pocket, gripped in my fist. Our exit was blocked, our nature vacation threatened by wild secrets. My wife breathed heavy in my ear. I wanted her to ask me to use my true wilderness knowledge to save us. She didn't ask. I wouldn't have known anyway. The wilderness seemed so far away, blocked by glass doors and Styrofoam rocks and a taxidermy fox with an ax to grind.

Instead of using my knowledge, I let my body lead. I left my family, adrenaline spilling through my thighs, and jogged toward the Employees Only cave behind the sales counter to beat the pulp out of the idiots behind it all. The rumbling noise from the exhibit thundered closer as I crouched into the cave. The deeper I went, the lower the ceiling dropped. I flattened to my belly against the cold tile floor. I slithered through the darkness headed toward a red light. I hoped the red light signaled management. I'd maybe show the owner's jaw my fistful of change.

The red light grew stronger. Mechanical chugging groaned through the walls. My back ached as I pulled myself along another few feet. What would it solve, coming out the other end to pound on the man in charge? The owner, making five hundred copies of the same flyer to slap onto the same damn car in the lot, futile as a raccoon gnawing at its neck to free itself from a trap. I didn't want to confront this man—a man I knew too well. But I pressed on, into the very guts of the beast.

I passed the red light throbbing over my head where the cave funneled tightest. I squeezed into darkness, through a flap, and then a bright light struck me. There he was, standing before a mirror, over a small sink, shaving the last strip of stubble from his throat. He wore a white shirt, buttons open, his bare chest exposed, a tie draping his collar, yet to be knotted.

"We're not paying to leave," I said, still lying on my belly, my back aching worse than before.

When he turned, I saw him bleeding from a nick on the neck. He looked murdered.

"Suit yourself," he said and clicked his razor against the sink bowl. The mirror before him opened to eye-splitting daylight. But it did me no good. I refused to bring my family past this murdered man, this final exhibit of failure. I retreated before the man shaved himself clean, buttoned his shirt, knotted his tie around his bleeding throat.

Back at the lobby, Trent said, "I think I got this one." He stroked his chin. "If fawns like quarters and bears like twenties…"

"Then foxes must eat dimes," Judy blurted from my wife's arms.

"Of course," my wife said. "But we're going to need a lot of them. A whole fistful at least."

I was lost. It didn't matter. I could worry about all the things

I didn't know later. I pulled out my fistful of change and slugged dimes into the fox's neck slot. Maybe the coins would slide down a chute, tink onto the desk of the owner. Maybe it would be a hailstorm of second chances, tapping out enough gas money to leave. My wife rubbed my shoulders, and my kids counted out each dime I spent, until finally the fox lifted back into the ceiling.

As we walked through the parking lot, I patted the kids on the back, wished I had words to express my pride better. My wife slathered on more lip gloss and smiled brightly. They all wore the satisfaction of gained knowledge. As for me, I longed to get back on the road, reach the campgrounds by dusk and assemble our tent, stretch out the sleeping bags, and build a fire, a big one. The work I knew how to do. I'd stare into the fire and forget the coins in my pocket, the alternator parts waiting to be orphaned back at home. The campfire's orange tails would nip at the stars, blinding the night.

the silverback and mom

Dad's on his way out. I hope I can see the signs if this sort of thing ever starts up with my wife, but the signs are gradual. Nothing in life ever happens without warning. It comes on slow, like the leaks in the roof of my shop, like what happened with my mom and the silverback gorilla.

Every time Mom came to visit, we would go to the zoo with Kay and the kids. We always started with the polar bears, because they were out front. Trent liked to press his face against the glass when the cubs swam by and pretend the giant paws had thrashed his cheeks. Then we'd see the lions and the otters and the hippos, who always just floated lazily and looked like they might burst right through their own skin. And none of them gave us any trouble. Then we'd swirl through the aquarium and the reptile house.

At the monkey house we'd grow tense, the kids quiet. Mom would fiddle with her purse, clasping and unclasping, offering the kids breath mints and chewing gum determinedly. The orangutans and tamarins didn't bother us at all. Even when they pulled on their pieces we could all have a laugh when Judy asked what they were doing. It was cute and innocent. Those chimps got me, though. They would study us, scratch their chins in tandem with our thoughtful gestures, and I'd wonder who was really watching who. They didn't have to work for their food, and women in khaki jumpsuits cleaned up their messes daily. I had to sell alternators all day for my food. The grease never came out of my fingernails, and I had to pay men in navy blue jumpsuits to barely clean up after themselves.

And the chimps didn't have to deal with that silverback gorilla.

The gorilla cage was always the last part of our visit. There was a whole family in there. A harem of mothers, a dozen kids running around and slapping every patch of grass in sight, and one giant daddy, a long gray patch smeared across his back. When he saw us coming, he would knuckle over to the window and chuff clouds of breath at my mom. She'd pretend like she didn't notice, but her cheeks would redden and she'd start pushing the breath mints and gum more heavily. That was the first dozen visits anyway. I shrugged it off as animal instinct. But soon after, he took to pounding the glass so hard we could feel the vibration in our chests.

The last time we visited, he didn't pound. Instead, he waltzed up to the glass and pressed his outstretched palm against it. His fingers were huge, creased with deep black lines. It was like in the movies where the lovers end up separated by quarantine or jail or bulletproof glass and, they just want to pretend touching is an option. Mom obliged. She pressed her palm against his, and his eyes glossed over. Kay asked why I never did anything as romantic as that. I shrugged. The gorilla leaned over, plucked a dandelion, and held it up to my mom.

That was all it took: those glossy eyes, the deep lifelines in his palm, and a dramatic hand-on-glass pseudo-embrace. Mom was done for.

I blame Dad, really. He never wanted to make the four-hour drive, his ass anchored to the soft routine of his worn red recliner, the world flashing by in reverse on the History Channel. My kids only saw him on the holidays. They grew up in spurts to him. He caught the highlights. Crawling to walking, mumbling to talking, talking to cussing. Kay said I had to stop cussing around them, but I knew they'd hear it all soon enough. Dad didn't claim a stake in this or much of anything. It was just easier to send his wife to the zoo than to feign interest.

The next time Mom came to town, she wanted to go to the art museum, said she was tired of the zoo. I said that was fine. I was tired of the zoo, too, plus the kids were excited about the Rothko exhibit. They went crazy for those big blocks of color that looked like demon-possessed cotton candy. So we headed to the art museum, even showed up early. The kids climbed all over the Giacomettis, and I told them to get the hell off because Giacometti always made his sculptures with such feeble, scrawny legs that it seemed they might snap and crush them at any moment. Just as I was telling them they wouldn't get to see any goddamn Rothkos if they didn't get it together, my wife tapped me on the shoulder and pointed next to the Goyas. There, right next to that painting where Cronus is eating up one of his kids, my mom and the silverback from the zoo were making out. At first, I thought he'd finally pounded his way through the glass, tracked the scent of Mom's Lily of the Valley perfume, and was now devouring her in a fit of lust. But one of his hands cradled the small of her back, the other holding her cheek gently, just fingertips. She leaned into his grip, as if she wanted to be swallowed, fearless of his massive jaws. I'd never seen her kiss like this. Mom and Dad only ever pecked in public, in passing, like a high-five.

The kiss really got me going, and I was already plenty pissed about my kids nearly crushing themselves on the Giacomettis on top of a crap day at work, two customers in eight hours. You see, the problem is a new alternator costs about as much as repairing it at my shop. My guys told me I needed to get with the times and start selling new alternators, but I always say, Why replace what you can fix? That was my problem at work, and the silverback and Mom were my problem outside. I suppose problems have a way of snowballing, and that might have had something to do with how I reacted to the scene by the Goyas.

I ran to the Japanese room and grabbed a long spear with a red tassel and hurled it at the silverback. My kids screamed, and that gave him all the notice he needed to pluck the spear right out of the air and snap it between his fingers, his other huge hand still tenderly wrapped around Mom's waist. Kay shook her head, but I could tell she was at least a little impressed by his reflexes.

Mom looked pissed, but the silverback touched her shoulder and sauntered over to me. His bare feet made a sucking sound against the hardwoods. I never realized how huge he was until I saw him up close. Standing upright in his pleated slacks and three-buttons-undone white shirt, he was a giant. If I counted the tip of the beret on top of his head, I'm sure he would have passed the six-foot mark. I didn't count the beret. I tensed up, squeezed my greasy nails into a fist for defending Mom's honor, a fist for fighting off the fact that he cleaned up better than me.

I read at the zoo that from fingertip to fingertip his arms measured past eight feet, but he folded those lanky suckers behind his back and bowed. Mom rambled over his shoulder that they were serious and she wasn't going back to Dad. She asked could I just be civil for once. Like I was the wild one. I told that bowing gorilla I needed to see his ass outside.

When we got outside, a crowd of museumgoers turned their snapping cameras toward us. I was ready to throw down and wished he'd take off his beret and maybe his shirt because he looked too sophisticated, and I was wearing a NASCAR T-shirt and a pair of jeans. He kept walking, ignoring the museumgoers' oohs and aahs. I followed him across the street, over a vacant grassy lot that made me think of the Serengeti and how much it would hurt when he ripped my arms out of their sockets. But he kept going. We ended up at a little bar across the street that was full of weekend warriors just off of their shifts—guys that build houses and work in factories. We sat down on some stools with round cushions on top that rotated on a single steel bar. He gave me a spin, and I couldn't hold back a little chuckle. The place was dark, but there was a cut-out of a girl in a red bikini strung up in enough Christmas lights to make the whole place glow rainbows. He ordered me an IPA and himself a gin and tonic.

I tried to stay mad, but I never know what to do with silence. I ended up blabbing, telling him about the alternator shop. He gripped my fingers, squinted at them, picked at each knobby joint. He nodded his approval. My hands felt small and special in his massive ones, and I was proud my fingers knew how to fix such intricate pieces of machinery. The Tigers game was playing on the TV dangling over the bar, and I asked him if he ever moonlighted over at the Detroit Zoo, ever caught games on his days off. I laughed at the thought. He grunted, bobbed up and down on his stool. And I realized he sure as hell got to do whatever he wanted.

He was a gorilla, and he was free now, wasting his time with me. Then I knew those chimps really were the ones with the better setup. All simian forms had played it smarter than me. But he sensed that and stuck out his tongue, made a flatulating sound. What he meant was clear: True intelligence had to do with empathy and entrepreneurship, and I had that going for me in spades. Then he gave me another spin on the chair. I laughed harder this time. He bought me another IPA and spun around some of the other guys in the bar, and they laughed too. The whole place seemed happy as Christmastime, and that made me a little sad because I wasn't sure exactly how we'd split the time between Dad and Mom this year. But then he spun me around again, and I figured it would all work itself out.

    I was a bit drunk, so the silverback let me ride on his shoulders on the way back. Really, I could have walked back, but, wow, could he run. He sprinted right out into traffic and just missed getting us smashed by a city bus.

    When we got to the museum, the kids had their fill of Rothko, their mouths smudged with reds and purples and blues like midnight. They wanted to climb on the Giacomettis one more time, and that got me pissed off all over again because I'd already told them how dangerous it was. I only said no because I loved them. The silverback cooed to them and spread his arms wide. Judy and Trent ran right over and climbed up his back, clawed at his nice beret, straddled his biceps.

    Everything looked beautiful and red with the sun setting over the parking lot, and I leaned on my wife. She smiled and squeezed my shoulder. I thought about how I might as well just keep repairing alternators for as long as I could, because that was what I liked doing and I was good at it. The last museumgoers trudged back to the parking lot, cameras stowed. The show was over.

    I asked Mom for a breath mint, but really I wanted to hug her. It wasn't the IPAs either. This was sincere. This woman knew so much more than I did about when to make a change, and I admired her for that. She said she was out of breath mints and she didn't have gum either. So I just put my arm around her and Kay and we watched the kids swing and shriek from the silverback's outstretched wrists.

take your family to work day

It's Take Your Family to Work Day at the construction site. I fitted the kids with OSHA-approved hard hats: a little pink one for Judy and a blue one for Trent. Before our day gets started, they're already chasing each other through the twenty acres we'll be clearing, weaving in and out of the birches and pines, a swirl of blue and pink. The painter's eight-year-old daughter peeks out from a second-story window across the street, her face dusted white with primer, and the cement masons' kids peep over the foundation next to us to utter guffaws before they slip back below. They take this seriously, apply themselves to their fathers' trades. But am I embarrassed my kids are screwing around and having fun? Hell no.

When I holler for them, Judy comes back with a palm full of acorns. She holds them out to me like she found diamonds in the trees. Trent's got a handful of rocks he chucks through the low-hanging poplar leaves in a pouty sort of way. He's jealous of the acorns, wishes he'd made better choices in his foraging, but that's how it goes: Sometimes you regret what you pick, and then you're stuck with your decisions. Like me, stuck for years with my failing alternator business.

Judy sees me smiling at the acorns in her hand and asks, "How much you think these babies are worth?"

"Well, they're nuts, sweetie," I say. "So, not much street value, but the little forest creatures sure love them."

She shakes her head and then runs over to Mom and her silverback lover. She's giggling with him under the spout of my woodchipper.

"Hey," Judy says, "how much you give me for all these nuts? Dad said you'd be interested."

My face gets hot, and I'm wishing she would have just found boring rocks like Trent. When I said forest creatures, Judy got mixed up. Now it looks like I'm the ignorant oaf who doesn't know the difference between jungles and forests, squirrels and gorillas.

He reaches into a pocket of his cargo shorts, tight around his thick, black leg hair, and comes up with a huge hand full of pocket change. Judy trades him. He winks at me. Mom smiles behind him. Judy beams. What a guy. Trent throws a stone at a pine way too close to Judy, and I tell him he can sit in the damn truck until lunch if he can't deal with his choices. He gets teary, kicks the backhoe tires. My wife Kay takes his hand and tells him we all make bad choices. She always knows how to empathize, how to rightly teach the kids the lessons I bark out too quickly. I know my faults. I'm not proud of them. I know I have one hell of a partner on my side. We're like the silverback and Mom, a perfect pair.

My family has suffered, though. My wife had to endure the expectant smiles at cocktail parties when she told colleagues her husband repaired alternators, them waiting for the punch line, when, no, it was really just alternators. Last year, I went to Trent's school with all the other dads, had to follow up the civil engineer who donated a little model city to their classroom. They shooed the class hamster through the model city the whole time I talked about stators and sliprings and rotors. My lecture hardly garnered a glance. Trent wouldn't even look at me. And poor Mom helped me box up the shop when it closed, slapping packing tape over expectations that her son would make something of himself.

Now I run a landscaping crew. I sold the alternator shop and bought myself some backhoes, a stump grinder, a few chainsaws and mowers and shovels, and the chipper my crew named Gabby. There's plenty of work with the construction boom. Everyone wants a house right now, even more than a model city.

I line up the family a few feet behind Gabby before I start her up and make her roar. That's my crew's cue to go full force. We choreographed it all yesterday. They go at the forest with the backhoes and chainsaws and the stump grinder all at the same time, felling trees in perfect harmony. The backhoes converge just behind me and circle each other like Shriners in their tiny cars. It's beautiful, and they pull it off like champs, not like the old alternator crew who'd be playing euchre every time I stepped into my office.

With the backhoes doing figure-eights behind me, I shout over Gabby, explaining to the family how by lunch we'll have at least five acres cleared, which means room for twenty houses and twenty mommies and daddies and their babies. I lecture with exuberance and confidence, pointing with both hands to this machine or that one, telling them what they all do. I had planned my speech, spent last evening in front of a mirror rehearsing. I considered wearing a button-up shirt, maybe even a tie, for my presentation, but then I realized how stupid that would be. If a man can't be himself in front of his family, he's in a sad place.

Judy and Trent look so excited, like they might start chasing the backhoes, but I've raised them to know better than to mess with dangerous machinery, plus I just mentioned it in my lecture. Mom and Kay both clap. I feel redeemed for that terrible day in Trent's class.

The silverback stares out at my handiwork like a statue, mesmerized. He's the only one that ever truly appreciated my skill and entrepreneurship at the alternator shop. Here, he is speechless.

I ask who wants a ride in the backhoe and Judy and Trent's hands shoot up. I let them ride on Murray's lap. He's my best worker, the only one I brought over from the alternator shop, the one who'd be scrubbing the grease out of the walls when the others were jabbering about bowers and going it alone. Murray promises Trent he'll let him steer, promises Judy she can work the bucket. Off they go, swerving through the trees. My wife and my mom want to try their hands at the stump grinder, so I tell them, "Have at it."

That leaves the silverback and me watching over the work, everybody's shiny new hard hats gleaming in the morning sun. The lot creaks and cracks over machine growls as trees topple.

Judy and Trent's backhoe trucks over to us, and Judy drops the first load at my feet. They're catching on so quick, could be journeymen in no time, if they wanted. I jam pine boughs into Gabby's mouth, and the sappy minced tree shoots out Gabby's spout in a sawdust blizzard.

"What would you like to run? Anything you want. My tools are your tools."

The silverback thumbs his lower lip so I get a good view of his massive canines.

"Wanna feed Gabby? She's always hungry," I joke. I load another armful of boughs into the chipper. Some of the sawdust drifts, peppering the black hairs on his face like the streak of gray on his back, only this makes him look older instead of more majestic.

He releases his lip and it slaps over his chompers. He heads off toward one of the empty houses across the street. I jog after, telling him how no one lives there yet or anywhere in the subdivision. He can check out any one he wants, maybe think about buying one for him and Mom. Soon, a family in every home on this street.

He chooses our show house, a massive two-story with gleaming hardwoods and a big picture window overlooking our landscaping site. Once inside, he turns to me, takes my hands in his. My palms face us, my curled fingertips. And I can tell he's wondering if I miss the alternator shop at all. And, yes. Hell yes, I do. It was my place, my idea, my crew, our repairs. Last week, I drove by the old shop. I sold it to a lumber company that now stores two-by-fours and plywood and trim and molding—never a single customer, just storage. I'd craned my neck to watch the blue-painted bricks flash by and almost rear-ended a school bus. It always wads up my heart to see it. But I don't tell him this, just stare at my hands.

He has a way of reading me, though, as if he can feel the kinks in my neck. He pokes at a milky scar on my left thumb knuckle, the one I got fixing my seventh-ever alternator, a fancy job for a '67 Jaguar. I bled like hell, but I got that thing sparking again. I would've stuck with it, but landscaping pays the bills like alternator repair never would.

The silverback drops my hands, walks out the back slider onto the deck. He reaches his long arms to grab a nearby shrub and shakes it back and forth, rips it from the earth. And, yeah, I get what he's showing me: Anyone can knock down trees. Only a special few fix alternators.

Past his sawdust-frosted scalp, next door, one of the frame carpenters' kids climbs up a ladder with a power nailer in his hand, the red compressor cord thumping behind him like a dead snake, slapping his father who holds the ladder. I haven't thought about it since Mom met the silverback at the zoo last year, but now I remember that he has kids, too. When he's not with us, after hours, days off, he's working with them. Every day is Take Your Family to Work Day for him. I wonder if they miss him, wonder if they've found someone better to take his place off hours like we've done with Dad. Maybe they're too busy to miss him.

"I was the only fool dumb enough to keep fixing just alternators," I say, punching his arm.

He stares off at the country road, at a farmer's old Chevy chugging by. And I wonder too: Who will fix them now?

Loyalty sustained me. My customers always came back. Every few years when their alternators bit it, they came knocking on my shop door. I bet they'll be dropping by the lumber yard for years, cradling their broken alternators like sick dogs. Eventually, they'll make their way down to the auto parts store and get new ones. Not my problem anymore.

The silverback is gazing down at me now with those burnt-brown irises of his. A tiny version of me is on display, reflected in the aquarium of his eyes. A version of me that's doing a job that pays instead of one I love.

"What about you?" I say. "The zoo? You can't tell me you love that. Why would you be with us if you did?"

His cavernous nostrils flare. He thumps his chest, twice, three times, just like in the movies. He's good at it, acting like a gorilla. And that makes too much sense for me. He is a gorilla, and somehow I've forgotten. It's who he is, what he does. Then, what does his time with us mean?

Just as my mouth gets dry and coppery, he unbuttons his shirt, slips out of his cargo shorts. He neatly folds them up and places them into my hands like a trophy. He pats the pile. I understand something I wish I didn't—he is leaving.

"Working today?" I ask.

He drops to his knuckles.

"What about Mom? What about my kids? You're their personal hero."

He grunts. And I know that if they were here, my family, they wouldn't worry. This would all feel natural. Soon I'd be bringing them to the zoo to read about silverbacks off the plaque outside their cage.

"Is it my fault, why you're leaving?"

The silverback, now all black except for that gray patch shimmering down his back, reaches into his shorts I'm holding and retrieves the acorns Judy sold him. He drops them on top of the clothes, prods them so they roll against my chest, and then he knuckles down the porch steps.

At first I'm embarrassed for him walking around naked. But he's a gorilla. There's no naked for a gorilla, no shame for him to feel. He hurdles the chain-link fence and lopes off toward the soybean field, the one the builders have already bought up and will develop into a cul-de-sac after the farmers' last harvest. This is the last time I'll ever see the silverback silhouetted against stubby green sprouts.

Outside the kitchen, the framer's kid is comfortable on the ladder now, nailing down an A-frame his father supports with a small crane. The kid's face is shiny. He clamps his tongue between his lips and shoots a half-dozen nails home. I can't see the father, just the arm of the crane, but I bet he's beaming, real proud.

I don't know what I'll tell my kids, my wife and my mom, who has her sleeves rolled up past her shoulders now and is joking with one of my workers. They all act like nothing has happened. Maybe they've understood what he was all along. I'm the only one who didn't get it.

Trent and Judy ride in the raised bucket of the backhoe, hands over their foreheads like they're scouting from atop the mast of a great ship. The masons' kids chuckle and point, but my kids' imaginations go on forever. I hope they never lose that.

All I can imagine is no more trees, flat dirt, twenty acres, and a ghost house plopping down its foundation over where Mom grinds furiously at a stubborn stump. Perhaps she'll rise from the foundation, up into the kitchen, sopping tiredly at the dishes, making Dad's dinner.

In my hands, I feel the phantom weight of alternators, the smell of new gaskets. I miss that weight, that smell. I miss alternators and when I was the best at what I did.

I stash the silverback's clothes in the back of my truck and head over to the chipper. I kick at the wheels a few times, but my boots are steel-toed and I don't feel it. I'm still holding the acorns, and for a moment I consider tossing them out into the dirt, to sprout new trees around the stump Mom's ground into a dimple. Mom walks over and asks what I have in my hand, studies my fist, as if about to peel open my fingers. I want to lean into her shoulder, recite a list of my mistakes, but instead I say, "Just some acorns."

Hoping, like Judy, for wild treasure, I toss them into Gabby's mouth. We watch carefully. They zip through the blades. All that spits out is the same sawdust.

I greatly appreciate the generous editors at Word West. Working with Julia Alvarez and Joshua Graber and David Queen has been such a pleasure. It's a rare, precious thing to have one's work honored so fully, and I will forever be grateful.

Thanks to the editors at *Takahe* for publishing an earlier version of "Take Your Family to Work Day," and thanks to Michelle Ross and the editors at *Atticus Review* for publishing "Still Life."

This book would not have been possible without my dear friends and mentors at Bowling Green State University. I owe so much to my first readers Joseph Celizic, Brandon Davis Jennings, Aimee Pogson, Megan Ayers, Anne Valente, Stephanie Marker, Catherine Templeton, Matt Bell, and Jacqueline Vogtman. That's the best batch of writers anyone ever lucked into working with. Lawrence Coates and Theresa Williams, my splendid teachers, helped me shape these stories. Most of all, I'm grateful for my time with Wendell Mayo, who inspired these stories and fostered the weird and wild. Wendell was the greatest mentor, and I miss him and think of him with every single sentence I write.

Thanks to my lovely family, Dad and Holly and Heather and, of course, thanks to my mom, Linda Hoffman, who always filled our lives with wonder.

Grandma Evelyn and Grandpa Glee took me and my sisters to Call of the Wild in Gaylord, Michigan when I was a kid. These trips stuffed my head with taxidermy joy and inspired "Still Life." Anyone who visits northern Michigan will miss something special if they skip Call of the Wild.

Finally, none of this would ever be possible or matter nearly as much without my partner Carrie, and my two favorite little humans Evelyn and Alison.

CPSIA information can be obtained
at www.ICGtesting.com
Printed in the USA
BVHW031950171119
564070BV00029B/324/P